A History of Me

Adrea Theodore

Illustrations by Erin K. Robinson

NEAL PORTER BOOKS

HOLIDAY HOUSE / NEW YORK

To Mom, with love and gratitude
To my Olivia, with love and hope —A.T.

For extraordinary Madison.
Witnessing life through your eyes
will always be the most vibrant of inspirations. —E.K.R.

Neal Porter Books

Text copyright © 2022 by Adrea Theodore
Illustrations copyright © 2022 by Erin K. Robinson
All Rights Reserved
HOLIDAY HOUSE is registered in the U.S. Patent and Trademark Office.
Printed and bound in September 2021 at Toppan Leefung, DongGuan City, China.
The artwork for this book was created using digital techniques and abundant love.
Book design by Jennifer Browne
www.holidayhouse.com
First Edition
1 3 5 7 9 10 8 6 4 2

Library of Congress Cataloging-in-Publication Data is available on request.

ISBN: 978-0-8234-4257-7 (hardcover)

I was the only brown person in class.

So when we talked about slavery,
I could feel every eye staring at me
behind my back.

When the teacher talked about
picking cotton
and slave shacks
and sisters being sold away separately,
I wanted to slide out
of my seat and onto the floor
and drift out the door.

My mom had told me before
that her great-great-grandmother,
on her mother's side,
was born enslaved.
But she died young.
So we didn't know much about her.

And so I should be grateful
to go to school
and learn.

I was.
I loved to learn.

But . . .

I was the only brown person in class
when we talked about the struggle
for civil rights in America,
and Martin Luther King Jr.,
and marches,
and police dogs,
and water cannons.

On the playground
some girls giggled and
whispered and giggled
some more,
and pointed at me
and looked away
when I looked at them.

I wanted to slip off the swing
and seep into the ground,
not making a sound.

My mom had told me before
that her grandmother, on her mother's side,
was born free,
but only got to go to school for a little while,
'til the third grade.

And so I
should be grateful
to go to school
and learn.

I was.
I loved to learn.

I was in the third grade.
and I had just learned how
to multiply,
and how to write essays,
and how to think for myself.

But . . .

I was the only brown person
walking home from school
with a violin case in my hand
when that boy rode by
on his brand-new bike
and barked at me,

"If it wasn't for Lincoln,
you'd still be our slaves!"

I wanted to sprint away
after him and ask,

"Is that all you see
when you look at me?"

My mom had told me before
that she
grew up in the South,
and everyone in her school was brown
like me.

She saw "Whites Only" everywhere.
She wasn't mad.
That was just how it was.

She wanted to be a nurse.
She couldn't go to school for that.
So she moved up north.

And so I
should be grateful
to go to school
and learn.

I was.
I loved to learn.

I loved science.
I became a doctor
who writes poems
and loves music.

But . . .

. . . my daughter
was the only brown person in her class
when they talked about slavery and
when they talked about civil rights.

I told her that I was
the only brown person
in my class too.

And just because
no one ever mentions
courage, strength,
intelligence, or creativity,
that doesn't mean it isn't there.

So . . .

. . . she shouldn't
slide to the floor
or seep into the ground . . .

. . . but
sit up straight
and
fly high into the sky.

Because . . .

. . . what matters more
are those moments in the mirror,
when she asks herself,

"What do I see
when I look at me?"

And when she does,
I hope
she will see
that she is
free
to be anything
she wants to be.

A Note from the Author

When my daughter was in elementary school and learning about slavery, she was saddened to know that if she had been born during the time of slavery, she would not have been able to attend school with some of her best friends, who were white. She didn't want to be different from them. She wouldn't have wanted to miss the opportunity to learn. She inherently understood this injustice, but she didn't know why things had to be so unfair. It troubled her, and I could see this unfair, invisible, familiar weight upon her shoulders.

It struck me that, incredibly, some *thirty years* after I had attended elementary school, the way the subject of slavery was being taught was still causing harm to young black and brown children. In talking with parents of other children, I knew that my daughter wasn't alone in feeling the way she felt: less than, inferior, wounded.

A History of Me came about as a result of my thinking about my own experiences in school and how the history of my own family was intertwined with the history of Black Americans in this country. In so many situations, the humanity of Black Americans who had been enslaved was ignored along with their immeasurable strength and resilience. They found creative ways to learn and care for one another in spite of the system designed to oppress them. When given the opportunity (such as during Reconstruction) many were able to prosper. Much of the history that I learned as a child did not mention or stress these things or provide the opportunity to recognize their humanity. They were enslaved but they were first and foremost *people*, with thoughts and feelings and dreams and desires and pain and sorrow and joy, and so were their descendants!

Rather than feeling shame, as I did for many years, I hope that descendants of those enslaved can understand the rich legacy that is theirs. While there are still systems in place that may hinder us, it is my hope that we can look back with a sense of pride at our ancestors, at their struggle and their will to survive in spite of those horrific circumstances. What happens when you are proud of where you come from? *You are free to be who you are and become who you are meant to be.* This is my hope for my own child—and for all children.

I remain grateful to my parents, my grandparents, my grandparents' parents, and all others in my lineage, who made it possible for me to be here and be who I am today.

—A.T.

A Note from the Artist

Illustrating *A History of Me* made me feel the power and resilience of my ancestors and recognize how they transcended their experience to inspire and uplift. I couldn't help but think of what gifts had been passed down to me and how I could continue to inspire magnificence . . . especially for young brown and Black girls.

—E.K.R.